Stuart Trotter

The Potty Book

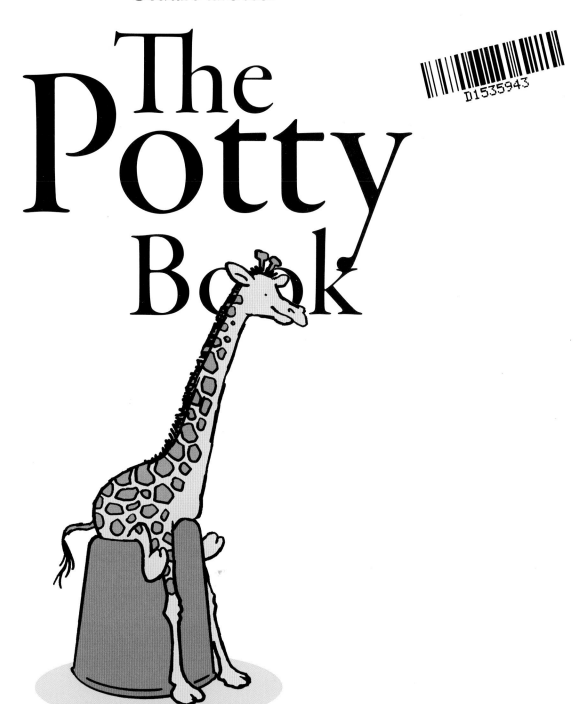

Is it a **bird**?
Is it a **plane**?
Is it a **UFO**?

No, it's **Captain Potty**,
He really has to go!

Fire engine potty,
Gleaming shiny red,
There for emergencies,
I park it by my bed!

There was
a little astronaut,
(while flying up to Mars)
who had to have her potty
time, floating in the stars!

Big teeth, long tail,
He really is enormous!
A creature from the distant past,
The scary

Pottysaurus!

Charlie is
a good boy,
He sits on
his pot,

But **Simon** tips it over
A good boy he's NOT.

"**Shiver me timbers!**"
Pirate Pete's afloat.
He's using his potty
just like it's a boat.

Princess Royal on the throne
It's all too plain to see,
It must have been the orange squash,
She needs a royal wee!

"Toot toot" potty,
Chugs down the line,
"Toot toot" potty,
The red one's mine!

I have the best seat in the house,
There's football on the TV.
But mom and dad are looking green,
I can't help being smelly!

Keep away, don't come close,
I'm really very spotty!
And now they've spread
from little body onto little potty!

"Giddy up potty!"
Says Cowboy Joe.
"Oh!" shouts mom
"Giddy up
and go!"

"The wheels
on my potty
go round
and round,
round and round,
round and round.
The wheels on
my potty
go round
and round,
All day long!"

I've sat here for far too long—I
think I need my mom.
She'll have to pull my potty off,
It's stuck tight to my **bum**!

A potty party,
everyone's happy...

...a potty party, 'bye bye' diapey!

First published in 2016 by © Rockpool Children's Books Ltd.

This edition published in 2016 by Rockpool Children's Books Ltd.
in association with Albury Books.
Albury Court, Albury, Thame
OX9 2LP, United Kingdom

Printed and bound in China

ISBN 978-1-906081-65-2 (Paperback)

rockpool
children's books